EZRA JACK KEATS
Louie

ISBN: 0-590-05611-5

Copyright © 1975 by Ezra Jack Keats. All rights reserved. This edition is published by Scholastic Book Services, a division of Scholastic Magazines, Inc., 50 West 44th Street, New York, New York 10036, by arrangement with Greenwillow Books, a division of William Morrow & Co., Inc.

12 11 10 9 8 7 6 5   0 1 2 3/8

Printed in the U.S.A.   07

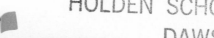

SCHOLASTIC BOOK SERVICES
NEW YORK · TORONTO · LONDON · AUCKLAND · SYDNEY · TOKYO

Susie and Roberto were putting on a puppet show.
They had spent a lot of time making the puppets.
Kids were trying to find seats next to their friends.
"Wow! Everybody's here!" said Susie.

For Florence B. Freedman

Louie

"There's Louie," said Roberto.
"I never heard a word out of him."
"Me neither," said Susie.
"Well, let's get started."

The curtain opened.
A mouse puppet appeared on the stage.

The mouse introduced Gussie.

When Louie saw Gussie, he stood up.

"Hey, sit down!"

"We can't see through you, Louie!"

"C'mon, sit down, will ya?"

Louie just stood and stared.

"Hello!" he said.

"What's going on?" asked Susie.
   Roberto peeked over the stage.
"It's Louie!" he whispered.
"He's talking to Gussie. He won't stop.
   What'll we do?"
   Susie thought for a moment.
"We'd better have Gussie answer him."

"Hi, Louie," Susie said in Gussie's voice. "Nice to see you. But me and the mouse gotta get on with the show. Will you please sit down? There's lots more to come." Louie sat down. The place got quiet and the play continued. The kids laughed at the adventures of Gussie and the mouse.

When the show ended, the puppets bowed.
Everybody cheered and clapped.
Louie jumped up and clapped loudest and longest.

As everyone was leaving, Susie and Roberto saw Louie.

"Would you like to say good-bye to Gussie?" Susie asked.

Louie grabbed the puppet and held on to it.

"What'll I do now?" Susie whispered to Roberto.

"Gussie is very tired," explained Roberto.

"She has to go home now."

Louie waited a minute, then let go of Gussie.

Susie and Roberto started off.

Louie waved until they were out of sight.

Then he walked home.

He went into his room
and sat on the floor.

He dreamed he was feeding Gussie
from a huge ice-cream cone.

Suddenly Gussie disappeared! And the cone, too!

Louie was falling

down

down

down

Now he was floating.
There were kids all around.
They were making fun of him.
"Hello, hello!"
"Nah—it's good-bye, good-bye!"
"Oh, yeah—hello and good-bye, Louie!"

"Louie," his mother called.

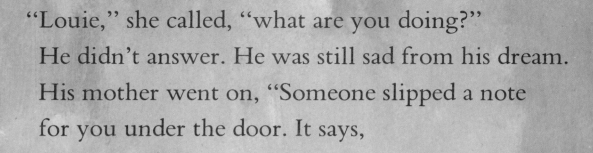

"Louie," she called, "what are you doing?"
He didn't answer. He was still sad from his dream.
His mother went on, "Someone slipped a note
for you under the door. It says,

    'Hello! Hello! Hello!
    Go outside and follow
    the long green string.'"

Louie got up and went outside.

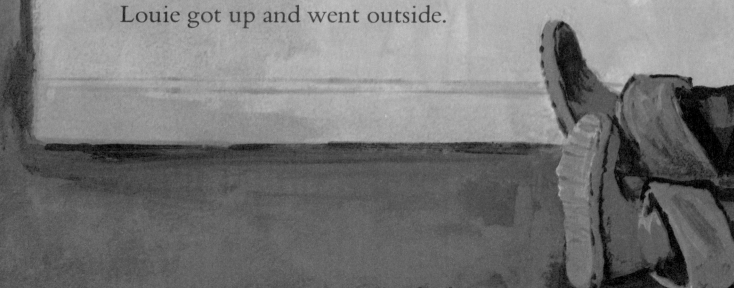